YOU DON'T CARE

THERE ARE ALWAYS TWO SIDES TO EVERY STORY.

TITLES IN TWO SIDES:

GIRL NEXT DOOR

Karen Moncrieffe

SAM

Emma Norry

YOU DON'T CARE

Luisa Plaja

STOP

Jenni Spangler

LOOKING AFTER MUM

Roy Apps

BRUISED

Donna David

Badger Publishing Limited, Oldmedow Road, Hardwick Industrial Estate, King's Lynn PE30 4JJ

Telephone: 01438 791037

www.badgerlearning.co.uk

YOU DON'T CARE

LUISA PLAJA

You Don't Care ISBN 978-1-78837-323-4

Publisher: Susan Ross
Senior Editor: Danny Pearson
Editorial Coordinator: Claire Morgan
Copyeditor: Cheryl Lanyon
Designer: Bigtop Design Ltd
Cover Illustration: Dave Robbins

6 8 10 9 7 5

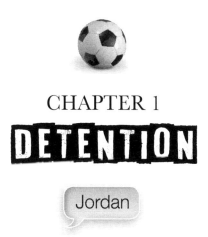

CHAPTER 1

DETENTION

Jordan

Cam is a mate but sometimes he annoys me.

It's lunchtime at school but we can't go out and play football. We are stuck in the cafeteria picking up litter. This is because Cam can't keep his mouth shut in lessons. It's always me he talks to. I always end up in detention with him.

The only good moment is when Hannah and her friends walk in. Hannah is in the year below and she's gorgeous. I can't help staring at her. When she looks in my direction, I trip and nearly fall over the black bin liner I'm holding. Hannah smiles at me.

Cam groans. "Jordan, you idiot!"

I ignore him. I'm pretty sure Hannah likes me. I think Cam is jealous.

"You know what everyone says about Hannah, don't you?" Cam asks.

"No. What?"

"I can't believe you haven't heard."

Cam thinks he knows everything. I pretend that I'm bored. "Go on, then. Tell me."

"She cheated on her last boyfriend. And the one before."

I fake a yawn. "So what?"

"So, she cheats on everyone. And she lies."

"That sounds like gossip to me. Fake news."

Hannah's friends walk out but she stops near the door. She smiles at me again.

This time I go over and say hello, dragging my bin liner with me. We chat for a bit and then I ask if she wants to meet me after school.

She thinks about it for ages. I nearly backtrack and tell her I didn't mean it.

Instead, I pick a banana peel off the floor, put it in the black bag and tell her a rubbish joke.

"Why did the banana go to the doctor?" I make my face all serious before I add the punchline. "It wasn't *peeling* well!"

Hannah's face lights right up. "That is terrible," she says. "The worst!"

I'm proud of myself. "I can tell you more."

"Please don't! You know what? I'll meet you later if you promise never to tell me a joke again!"

She wants to go out with me. Yes!

"Deal," I say, cool as anything.

"Deal," she repeats. "Oh, and Jordan?"

"Yes?"

"What kind of key opens a banana?"

I stare at her.

"A monkey!" She laughs. "I never said I wouldn't tell worse jokes." She grins as she walks away.

I go back to picking up litter.

Cam shakes his head at me. "She is bad news," he says.

I shrug. "I don't care."

*

Going out with Hannah is amazing. We get on really well. We have similar taste in films and music. She even supports the same football team as me.

Cam doesn't get it.

"I'm warning you, Jordan. She cheats and lies."

"She wouldn't do that to me. She likes me."

"Only until she meets someone more interesting," Cam says. "And everyone in the world is more interesting than you, mate!"

"Ha, ha!" I reply. I'm not worried. I'm the one she cares about. We're going out again today, after school.

My phone pings. It's Hannah saying she can't see me later after all.

Cam reads over my shoulder and gives me a knowing look. "She hasn't explained why she can't meet you. What's her excuse?"

"She's probably just busy."

"Busy with one of them, I bet!" Cam points at some lads walking past us. They're in the year above and they always beat us when we play them at football. "Isn't that one her ex?"

It is. But I won't let Cam get to me. He just wants to wind me up.

"I don't care," I say.

But I do, a bit.

CHAPTER 2

HOSPITAL APPOINTMENT

Hannah

"Hannah, I'm sorry," Dad says to me at breakfast. "Can you come straight home after school today?"

Oh. I was planning to meet Jordan again. "Why?"

I think I know the answer. Dad probably overdid it yesterday at my sister's Karate competition. I bet he pretended to be fine, chatting at the side of the hall with Nat's friend's dad.

Dad can't do too much without making himself unwell. I tell him to pace himself. He never listens to me.

"My hospital appointment got moved and I might be late. I know Nat can walk home by herself now that she's in Year 7, but..."

I know what Dad means. Nat is not like most 11-year-olds.

"Don't worry." I touch Dad's arm. "I'll look after her."

Dad gets up from his chair. On a good day, he can spring up and walk around as easily as me and Nat can. On a bad day, he struggles to move at all, or at least not without a lot of help from his special scooter. And some help from me.

Today is somewhere in between. He uncurls in slow motion like a snail coming out of its shell. His face scrunches with pain and effort. It hurts to watch him.

"Are you sure you can get to the hospital on your own?" I ask.

"Don't try to get out of school, Hannah!"

"I'm not!" I tell him. "But if you need me..."

He shakes his head. "I'll be fine. I'll call the hospital transport service if I need to. They can take me to the door of the waiting room."

"Promise me you will. Should I make Nat's lunch?"

Dad looks sad. "If you don't mind. I'm sorry, love."

"It's OK, honestly."

I pull out the bread I bought yesterday on the way home from school. I slice it the way my sister likes. Nat can be really fussy. She has horrible meltdowns when things are not what she expects. She can't help it, though. She does well to cope as much as she does. I know school is really hard for her. She can't always deal well with all the noise, brightness and people.

I worry about the filling. I forgot to buy Nat's usual tomatoes and we only have cherry ones.

Nat does eat those sometimes, but I can't remember how she likes them. I don't want to bother Dad with it. Mum always knew what to do. I miss her all the time.

Dad is watching me. "Slice each one down the middle, once," he says. "Thank you, Hannah."

I know Dad misses Mum too. I blink a lot. I don't want him to know I feel sad.

I'm so busy getting everything ready, pushing Nat out of the door and off to school on time that I totally forget to text Jordan to say I can't meet him. I have a club at lunchtime and I won't see him during the day.

It will have to wait until break time. He'll understand.

I didn't really rate Jordan at first, but I think it was only because he hangs around with Cam. I don't like Cam at all. I know him a bit because my sister goes to Karate club with his sister.

He asked me out once and I said no. After that, he called me names. I can live without boys like him. He reminds me of my ex — he turned out to be a loser, too.

Jordan seems different. He was clumsy and sweet when he first talked to me. He tried so hard to make me laugh.

Most of all, I enjoy spending time with Jordan. He makes me feel normal. I'm always busy with shopping, cooking and helping my family. It's difficult to fit in my homework and even harder to find time to have fun.

My friends all understand when I can't go out, or when I have to rush home. But I don't like it when they feel sorry for me. I do it because my family needs me. Anyone would do the same.

Jordan doesn't feel sorry for me at all. He doesn't even know about my dad or my sister. Cam won't have told him. He thinks my family is weird. I heard him say that to someone at Nat's Karate club.

I don't want Jordan to know too much about my home life. It might change everything. But I'll have to say something sooner or later.

CHAPTER 3

TOTALLY HEALTHY

Jordan

When I see Hannah at school the next day, I ask her why she had to cancel our date.

She doesn't answer me right away. I ask her again.

She hesitates. "My dad needed me," she explains at last. "I had to look after my little sister."

"That sounds annoying." I'm an only child so I don't really know, but Cam always complains about his sister. Nothing about having a sibling sounds good.

"Not really." Hannah takes a deep breath. "You see, my dad has an illness. I have to help a lot at home. But it's not a problem."

"Oh. Why didn't you tell me before?"

Hannah shrugs. "I don't like talking about it. My family is normal, really."

I put my arms around Hannah. She smells amazing. And she's a great person. I knew Cam was wrong about her.

But when I talk to him about it later, Cam looks grim. "She stood you up because her dad is ill? Is that what she told you?"

"Yes. Why?"

"Nothing, mate. Nothing," Cam says, shaking his head.

"No, go on. What's the problem now?"

"Sounds like an excuse to me."

Cam is annoying me again. "What are you on about?"

"Our dads know each other. Hannah's weird sister does Karate with my sister. They were chatting to each other at the sports centre just two days ago."

"So?"

"So, I was there too. And Hannah's dad looked fine to me. Totally healthy."

"She said he was in a lot of pain yesterday."

"Really? There was nothing wrong with him the day before. He was with my dad the whole time. Dad always says he wishes he could sit down, but Hannah's dad had no problem with standing for ages," Cam says. "I'm sorry, mate. I think Hannah made this whole thing up."

"That makes no sense. Why would she lie?" We walk down the sports corridor towards the maths room.

"Why do you think?" Cam nods at the wall. There's a photo of the football team in the year above us. It's from when they beat us in the final. Hannah's ex is in the centre of the picture, holding a shiny cup.

"You're wrong, Cam."

"I hope so. For your sake."

All the way through maths I think about it. Cam knows Hannah's family much better than I do.

He is getting to me, after all.

*

I see Hannah the next day at lunch. She sits next to me and gives me one of her lovely big smiles.

I don't smile back. "Cam says his little sister does Karate with your sister."

"Yes. Those two are always beating each other up." Hannah laughs. "Sometimes I worry about them. Or about Nat, anyway. That's my sister. She loves fighting!"

"Cam says his dad knows your dad."

"Yes. From Nat's Karate club."

"He says your dad chatted to his dad, standing at the side of the hall."

"Yes, probably." Hannah gives me a strange look. "Why? What's the matter, Jordan?"

Maybe I shouldn't listen to Cam.

"Nothing," I say.

Hannah eats her lunch.

I'm not hungry. I still want to know whether Hannah has been telling me the truth, but I don't know how to ask.

"I've got a big match next week," I say instead. We're playing the year above — the team with

Hannah's old boyfriend.

Hannah nods. "I heard about that."

"Did you? Who told you? Someone from the other team?" Her ex?

She gives me a strange look. "Everyone knows. It was announced in Tutor Group. My friends are all going."

That sounds true.

"Will you be there too? Maybe we could go out afterwards?" I suggest. "There's that new pizza place in the High Street."

"Why not?" Hannah smiles at me. "Sounds like fun!"

I hope Cam is wrong.

CHAPTER 4
MOBILITY SCOOTER

Hannah

I might be a carer but I'm not an angel. The house phone rings and I pick it up and say, "What?" in a bored voice. I know I sound rude.

Dad wants me to be polite, but people who call the main phone are always trying to sell things we don't need.

"Mr Brown?"

Do I sound like my dad? I don't think so. "He can't come to the phone right now," I say. I've only just got home from school and the house is very quiet, so I think Dad must be sleeping. Nat will be late because she has Maths Club after school. My sister adores maths.

The voice on the phone says, "We're running some special deals on windows..."

I end the call. Who has time for this?

It rings again straight away. "We don't want your windows!" I bark into the phone.

"Hannah?"

"Dad? Is everything OK?"

I already know it's not. He hasn't told me off for being rude.

Dad sighs. "I'm really sorry, love. Can you look after Nat for a bit when she gets back today?"

"Today?" I repeat.

It's the day of Jordan's big game. I have to be at the school field soon, ready for the kick-off. I was looking forward to hanging around with my friends, and having pizza with Jordan afterwards.

Sometimes I hate my life.

I take a deep breath. "Where are you, Dad? What's going on? When will you be back?"

"Soon, I hope. I'm at the shops. But I had to sit down for a little rest."

I look around. Dad's mobility scooter is parked near the front door. That's why I thought he was at home. "Did you walk to the shopping centre?" I already know the answer.

"Yes. I thought I could nip to the supermarket. Give you a break." Dad's speaking slowly. I think he's in pain.

"I went shopping yesterday, Dad!"

"You forgot Nat's special bread," Dad says.

I want to shout at him. "She can live without it!"

"You know it's not that simple."

"She's not a little kid anymore!"

"Hannah..."

Why am I angry with my dad? It's not his fault I forgot the bread.

"Don't worry, Dad. I'll look after Nat. You take care, OK?" I end the call.

A little while later, the door opens. It's Nat. She's early, and I can tell she's in a terrible mood."I hate everyone!" she shouts.

I was right. "What's the matter? Why are you home already?"

"Maths Club was cancelled! Because of a stupid football game! Everyone wanted time to get ready. They all want to go, including our teacher. But I don't!"

"Nat, it's OK."

"No, it's not! Maths Club is the only good thing about school!" Nat stamps her feet.

"Tell you what, Nat. I'll make you a sandwich." Food sometimes calms my sister down. But then I remember that I forgot her bread. "I'll have to use different bread, though, OK?"

The phone rings. I ignore it.

My sister puts her hands over her ears and shouts, "No!"

Ring, ring. Shout, shout.

I want to scream.

I answer the phone. "Yes?" It had better not be about selling windows.

"Hello?" It's a woman's voice. "Hannah Brown? I'm calling from the hospital. We have your father here."

Oh no. "Is he OK?"

"Yes, don't worry. He had a fall at the supermarket. We just need to check him over." The woman gives me more information.

I need to go to Dad. But I can't leave Nat.

I can't take her with me, either. There's no way she can cope with a hospital right now.

My sister is still shouting with her hands over her ears, "No, no, no!" I need to calm her down before it gets any worse.

I take a deep breath and stroke her arms, gently pulling them down to her side, just like Dad taught me. I grab her stress ball from the kitchen counter and place it in her hand, telling her to count slowly to ten.

After a while, the storm seems to pass and she is able to talk to me again.

"Nat, listen to me," I say. "Your friend from Karate Club lives near us, doesn't she?" She's Cam's sister, but that doesn't matter.

"You mean Emily?" my sister asks. "She's nice. I don't hate her."

"Would you like to go to her house for a bit?"

"Yes!" Nat smiles at last. "But I don't have her number."

I have Cam's number, though. He gave it to me before I knew what a loser he was.

"Hold on."

I call Cam and explain everything. He says Nat can come round. "I'm on my way to the football, but my parents are home," he says. "I'll call them. They won't mind. They love it when Emily has friends over." He tells me his address.

Maybe he's not so bad after all.

We catch a bus to Cam's house and I leave Nat with Emily and her parents. Then I take another bus to the hospital.

CHAPTER 5

THE MATCH

Jordan

On the day of the match, I'm more nervous than I should be. I want to beat the current champions more than ever. I want to prove to Hannah's old boyfriend that *I* am the best.

I want Hannah to think so, too.

"You coming out with us later?" Cam asks in the changing rooms. "We're planning to celebrate our big win!"

"No, you go ahead without me. I'm seeing Hannah after the game."

Cam snorts. "What makes you think she'll be here?"

I'm getting fed up with him. "We planned it. She said she'd come and watch me."

"Watch you, or the other team? Like her ex-boyfriend?" He pulls his shin pads on. "Or maybe she won't come at all."

"She will." I tie my laces tighter than I need to. "She promised."

At half time, we're losing 3–0 and there's no sign of Hannah. I look everywhere for her before we head in for our team talk. I recognise her group of friends, but I don't see her.

Cam is in the changing room, sitting as far away from Mr Clark, our coach, as he can possibly get. I slump next to him. Mr Clark starts lecturing us about how bad we were in the first half.

"Told you Hannah wouldn't come," Cam whispers to me. He always ignores the coach if he can get away with it. "Didn't I tell you?"

"You did." I feel rubbish. "Maybe something came up. But she might still meet me afterwards..."

"No, mate. She has moved on," Cam says. "But she'll tell you she couldn't make it because of her dad. She'll keep pretending her dad is ill even though he's fine. It's a great excuse, isn't it?"

I wish Cam would shut up.

"Jordan, mate." Cam looks around at our teammates. They are all staring sadly at their boots. "Has Hannah even bothered to tell you she couldn't make it? Has she called you? Or sent you a text?"

I feel a rush of anger. Cam is right. Hannah said she would be here. If she changed her mind, why didn't she say so?

"Don't be a loser. More of a loser. Not if you can help it," Cam says.

When the team talk is finished, I check my phone but there's no message from Hannah.

It's true. Hannah doesn't care.

"OK. I'm finishing it," I say to Cam. I type a message to Hannah, breaking up with her. I do it quickly before I change my mind.

Cam cheers me on. "You tell her!"

I send the message. I stride back onto the pitch. I feel strong and in control.

I also can't stop thinking about her. I'm totally distracted. The other team scores two more goals against us and I barely notice. I hope I've done the right thing. I —

"Jordan!"

It's our coach.

"Jordan, you're offside!" he shouts. "Where is your head?"

Mr Clark has a point. I try to get back in the game. Instead, I trip over my own feet. I fall to the ground with a horrible thud.

I can't move.

I don't know what hurts more.

My leg, twisted under me.

Or my heart.

CHAPTER 6

HOSPITAL

Hannah

It's really crowded at the Accident and Emergency department. I have to wait a long time to speak to a member of staff. She takes my details and tells me to sit down while they find my dad for me.

After a while, the automatic door swishes open. I'm surprised when Mr Clark, our school sports teacher, walks in. He's pushing a wheelchair. There's a boy sitting in it. He's wearing a football kit.

I'm even more surprised when I see who the boy is.

It's Jordan!

I don't know whether to speak to him or not.
I can't believe he broke up with me by text,
without even giving me a chance to talk to him.

Before I can decide what to do, a nurse speaks to
me. "Hannah Brown?" she asks.

I nod.

Maybe Jordan hears my name because he looks
around and notices me. His eyes grow wide.

I turn away from him.

"Follow me," says the nurse. "I'll take you to
your dad."

Dad is in a side room. He's lying in a trolley bed
and looking pale, but not too bad.

"I'm so sorry, Hannah. Have I ruined
your evening?"

I can't answer that honestly. I don't want to upset him. "Are you OK, Dad?"

"A bit shaken up. I was lucky, though. I don't think anything's broken!"

"Good," I say.

"They're going to take some x-rays, just to make sure."

I nod. "Good," I repeat.

"I promise I won't do it again, Hannah. Walking to the shops, pretending everything is fine. Next time I'll take the scooter."

"You do that," I say. I can't have a go at him. He looks too sad.

"Listen to us, Hannah! Sometimes I wonder who's the adult and who's the child," Dad jokes.

I don't laugh. It's not funny.

Instead, I give Dad a hug.

I go with Dad to the x-ray room but I'm not allowed inside. I find the waiting area.

Jordan is there, still sitting in a wheelchair. I don't know where Mr Clark has gone.

"Hi," he says.

I can't exactly avoid him. "Hello, Jordan."

"So it's true about your dad?" he asks.

"What do you mean?"

"He's really ill?"

I stare at him. "What?"

"Cam said you were lying. He said..." Jordan stops talking. He looks at me. "It's almost like he didn't want me to go out with you."

"Cam asked me out once, a while ago," I tell him. "I said no. He's been a pain ever since. Only he did help me earlier, when I called him about my sister."

"You called him? Today?" Jordan's voice gets louder. "Is something going on between you?"

Oh, please. "Jordan, it's not like that." I think about it. "Wait, why didn't he tell you I called him? It was before the match started. He could have explained that I had an emergency."

Jordan frowns. "Why did you call Cam and not me?"

I frown back at him. "Why did you believe Cam and not me?"

There's a long silence. Then Jordan looks into my eyes. "You're right," he says. "I can't believe he's done this. I shouldn't have listened to him. I'm sorry, Hannah. I really am. Can we try again? Can we still see each other?"

I shake my head.

"Bye, Jordan," I say. "I hope your leg is OK."

He looks sad. "Bye, Hannah."

When my dad is ready, I wheel him back to the main room and call the hospital transport to take us home. I ask them to pick up Nat on the way. I'm happy that Cam's not home when we get there. I don't want to speak to him.

Nobody knows what my life is like. Nobody really understands. Some people try, and the ones who don't aren't worth my time.

But I'm strong. I can do this. I smile at my dad and sister.

We have each other and we will be fine.

Young Carers

What is a Young Carer?

A Young Carer is someone under the age of 18 who helps look after someone in their family who is ill, or who helps by looking after the rest of the family while the sick person can't.

How many people are Young Carers?

It's estimated that there are around 700,000* Young Carers in the UK. That's about one out of every twelve secondary-school-age students.

What do Young Carers do?

Young Carers find themselves with more responsibilities than other young people. They are likely to have to do more household chores than is usual. They may also provide emotional support to the person they are caring for; or learn how to nurse them or look after their personal needs, like bathing and dressing.

*2017 figures

What kind of problems do Young Carers face?

Young Carers often have less free time than other young people. Sometimes their friends don't understand this. It can be stressful, worrying and tiring being a Young Carer, too. They may find that they have less time to themselves, or to do their homework. Sometimes, it can be hard to concentrate at school.

The Carers Trust

The Carers Trust offers help and advice for Young Carers. They also organise an annual Young Carers Awareness Day.

You can visit their website:

www.carers.org/about-us/about-young-carers

Or contact them at:

Info@carers.org

ABOUT THE AUTHOR

Luisa Plaja grew up in Sicily and London speaking Italian and English, sometimes at the same time. This made her confusing but it also ignited her passion for words and language.

As a teenager, Luisa submitted photo romance scripts to her favourite magazines, and some of her stories were published. She caught the writing bug and has since written many novels, short stories and non-fiction books, available in more than ten languages. She has also worked as a television subtitler, dictionary editor, technical translator and linguistic software developer.

Currently living in Devon, Luisa has always been an avid reader and recommender of Teen/Young Adult fiction.

I'm nearly at the hospital when I remember to text Jordan. He got a bit funny with me last time I had to cancel. I hope he will understand.

My phone is deep inside my bag, where I threw it in my hurry to sort out Nat.

When I find it, there's a message waiting. It's from Jordan.

He's breaking up with me.